W9-BZU-137

A PERFECT BLANK

RYE DURAN

An imprint of Enslow Publishing

WEST 44 BOOKS™

Please visit our website, www.west44books.com.
For a free color catalog of all our high-quality books,
call toll free 1-800-542-2595 or fax 1-877-542-2596.

Cataloging-in-Publication Data

Names: Duran, Rye.
Title: A perfect blank / Rye Duran.
Description: New York : West 44, 2020. | Series: West 44 YA verse
Identifiers: ISBN 9781538382851 (pbk.) | ISBN 9781538382868
  (library bound) | ISBN 9781538383438 (ebook)
Subjects: LCSH: Children's poetry, American. | Children's poetry,
  English. | English poetry.
Classification: LCC PS586.3 D873 2020 | DDC 811'.60809282--dc23

First Edition

Published in 2020 by
Enslow Publishing LLC
101 West 23rd Street, Suite #240
New York, NY 10011

Editor: Caitie McAneney
Cover Design: Sam DeMartin
Interior Design: Seth Hughes

Photo Credits: Cover (background) Wangwukong/The Image
Bank/Getty Images; cover (man) Yagi Studio/Taxi Japan/Getty
Images.

Printed in the United States of America

CPSIA compliance information: Batch #CS18W44: For further information contact
Enslow Publishing LLC, New York, New York at 1-800-542-2595.

For those sweet freaks on the outside
who start the revolutions

A Blank Beginning

I remember the day
I was born.

This is important
because I was not born
the way other
babies are born.
And I was not born
to be like
other babies.

The room was so
bright. There were
nine others. Exactly nine
others born that day. Nine
like me. None like me.

A speaker boomed
over each of us.

From my speaker
came a voice.
And that voice
said *Alex, Alex, Alex, Alex, Alex, Alex.*

Project Apogee

In the beginning
before us, before the voice
that said my name,
there was a crisis. People
were dying. There was so much
suffering. There wasn't
enough food or medicine
to go around. We were made
to be the solution.

Ten perfect
babies. The hope
of humanity. We would
never get sick. We would
never feel depressed. Never get
distracted from doing
our homework. We would
win every contest.

And then we
would be leaders.
Diplomats. Award-
winning scientists.
Inventors. We
would be smart
and strong. We would lead
humanity
back from the edge
of collapse. You know,
hero stuff.

But in the beginning
we were just
babies.

And that's a lot
of pressure to put on
a baby. Even
a perfect baby.

The Nine

Let me tell you
about the others.

They were
my family because
we all came from
the same place,
which is nowhere.

We were made
in a lab.
Made by scientists working
for the government.
Each scientist working
on Project Apogee
named one of us.
They became responsible
for our growth
as our Monitor.

And so
A is for
all of us:

Ander who is
by minutes the oldest.
The most stubborn.
Weirdly also
the sweetest.

Ander is full
of care for
his fellow man. He will
make a good president.

Aggie is a musical
mastermind. A child
composer, like Mozart.

She finished her first
symphony at four and a half.
Plus, she outranked
the rest of us
in strength
that same year.
And every year since.

Ashlun has been
in commercials
since he was
in diapers. His face
has been studied
for its
perfect balance.

Ace is the problem-solver.
The puzzler.
She was making
board games for four
major toy
companies by ten
years old.

Asa has traveled
with the National
Ballet Company
as a dancer and
acrobat.

Abel has
amazing blood.
Which means
he is the
healthiest person
in the world. He
will live longer
than any human
ever has.

Ada is
a coder. She beat
every video game
the Monitors
could find. She was called in
by the government.
Helped with the famous
cyberattacks of 2031.

Alo is a diver. He has
the world record
for holding
his breath. Seventeen
minutes upside down.
Alo is a survivalist.
He can go for 12
days without water.

And finally, there is
Anto. She is a poet.
And she
is the only one
who spoke
to me when
I was kicked out
of Project Apogee
eight years ago.

I Am Alex

I am Alex
and I remember
everything.

The Ten at Two

Years one and two
we lived in a wing
of Project Apogee
called the Rainbow Ring.

Each of our
rooms was painted
a single color,
a color chosen to be
our color. A color
to bring out
our gifts.

My color was blue,
but not blue like my
eyes. Bluer. Starting
with my room, I was
meant to remember
every blue shape
I saw. For the rest
of my blue life.

Anto lived next door.
A purple room
filled with
purple pillows
and soft things.

Ander's world
was fire-engine red.
He lived
with a little red robot.
It taught him
to make jokes
in four languages.

My blue room
was the emptiest of all
the rooms. To make
space, they said. Space for my
brain to fill with dreams
and eventually
memories.

There was a little
projector that moved
clouds across the ceiling
during the day. It made
star patterns
at night.

I must tell you about
Myra. She was my
Monitor. She gave me
my name.

The blue room was always
filled with her face.
Her smile.
I remember her
teeth. She had a
large gap between
her front teeth.
She could whistle
through the space
in her mouth.

She held me
and rocked me
in a blue chair
while the ceiling
turned clouds to stars.

And she would say,
"Time to go
inside, baby."
And by *inside*,
she meant
the place inside my head.
It was already better
and more beautiful
than anything outside.

My Left Leg

Everyone else walked
before I walked.

But Dr. Pinker
told Myra, who told me,
it was just because
I was doing
what I was
built to do.

I was busy
remembering
everything.
Like a photograph
or a perfect record
of every moment.

Walking was just not
important to me. And that
was fine
at first.

I could swim
beside Alo.

I loved
to dance with Asa.

I could lift almost
as much as Aggie.
But still I could not run.

My left leg was
shorter and weaker than
my right leg. And my foot
sometimes curled in
and trembled.

Sometimes when Myra
wasn't around, Dr. Pinker
tried to trick my legs
by shocking me with
a stick that he plugged
into the wall.

My Blue World

Year three
was the first year
I failed
to grow
as the Project expected
I'd grow.
A red flag
in my blue world.

Many Kinds

At the end of year three,
Project Apogee
gave us to our parents.

Saying goodbye to Myra
was the hardest part
of going to live
with my parents.

But she came
to visit us
every weekend.
She brought
new books and pictures
for me to memorize.

She would ask,
"How many
oranges were
on the ground
before?"
And I
would tell her.

And my parents
would cheer and
peel oranges
for smell. Which
Myra told them

helped my memory work
even better.
I went to physical therapy
three times a week.
I started to move
a little faster. A little better.

But average-kid-better.
Which Myra told me
for Project Apogee kids
is not better
at all.

I cried sometimes
because I was not
getting better.
And I would not
get better.

I would not
ever be the kind of good
I was supposed to be.
When I cried, Myra
would say sorry over
and over again.
And she would
remind me,
"There are many
kinds of fast."

Making Fun

When I started school
I got a chance to meet
"average" kids.

They were
meaner, slower,
and louder than
Project Apogee kids.

My very first day, the teacher
told me to introduce myself.
So I told the class
everything I knew
about my blue world.

I told them
how many
kinds of birds
lived in our
backyard.
And what they
liked to eat.

Then I talked for a while
about which ones
flew south

for the winter and why.
There was a table of kids
in the back
who laughed. They talked through my
report on blue jays.

At lunch
a nice girl named Charlie said
she was sorry
they were making fun
of me. I asked, "What is
making fun?"

Average Kids

I learned that average kids
thought I was weird. Weird for
the exact same reasons
Project Apogee thought
I was good. They did
not like my memory. Or
the way I talked about
the things I remembered.

I felt embarrassed. Like
I didn't know which parts
of me to hide. This feeling
was a new kind
of memory.

The Ten at Seven

At the end of year seven
we returned to
Project Apogee for
a month
to test our
progress.

The Ten of us had not seen
each other more than once
a year since we were
adopted.

I had missed Anto
so much.

And the others. We were
connected in a way
that was familiar.
I felt so close to
them, so understood.

Back at Apogee

we returned to our old
rooms, where there
were new beds.
New toys and books.
But my room
was as blue as ever.

And the night sky
where the stars
had glowed above
me while I
slept—each
group of stars
now had
a name.

A screen on my
nightstand let me
pick. Ursa Major,
the great bear. Or Sagittarius,
the archer. Whichever
star group I chose
would glow even
brighter against
the rest.

My blue dreams
came back to me right away
that first night. I dreamed
of a blue meadow
full of blue flowers
that turned
toward the full moon.

Family of Ten

The Ten of us
had dinners together
in the common room.
We had an hour
in the morning
and an hour
before bed to
talk to each other.

We shared our
stories of home.

Ander said
that he, like me,
was an only child.

Anto talked
nonstop about
all of her
little brothers and
sisters. And her
favorite person
in the world—her
grandmother.

"She's a witch,"
she said. And
we all wanted
to know
what that meant.

We talked about
our schools. How
much more we liked
each other
than the rest of
the kids we knew.

Alo was homeschooled.
And his family took lots of
trips to other countries
and museums.

Some of us
were jealous. "It's OK,"
Alo said, "but they never
leave me alone."

Ada said, "I know exactly
what you mean. My family
lives with a bunch
of other families.
We all work
the land
together."
I had never
heard of such a thing.

"It's my job," Ada said,
"to take care of
feeding the
animals. So I built an
automatic system
that delivers
food to the chickens
at the right
times."

We talked about
how different
we all were
from each other.

And how much
the same.

The Stars and the Gods

One night, Anto snuck
into the blue room.
I was sure
we would get caught.
She wrapped
her super soft
purple blanket around
us both.
And snuggled close.

She told me that
her grandmother
would sometimes
talk about
how one day they
would run away
together. Just
the two of them.

And live
free.

"She says this place
is the opposite
of free," Anto told me.

I told her
how so many of
the stars were
named for people
who the gods
were punishing
for being
too powerful. These
regular people
who the gods
thought had become
too much
like the gods.

"That's funny,"
Anto said, "because
the gods
made them."

Then
she went back
to her purple room
and left me
to my blue
dreams.

One Blue Dream

I had one
blue dream
of a blue god.

The blue god
was angry.
So he turned me
into a blue star
that no one
could find
in the huge
black night sky.

Dr. Pinker's Lab

On the way
to my first
physical test
the next
morning, I saw
Myra in the hallway
outside
Dr. Pinker's lab.

She was
talking to
Dr. Pinker's
assistant, Glen.
He was big and square
and always looked
like he had just smelled
something bad.

She looked
worried. But she
smiled at me. She
smiled one of those
worried smiles
so I knew
something
was wrong.

In the lab, Myra sat
across the room
with a clipboard
and watched
Dr. Pinker and Glen
watch me.

"Hello, Alex. Please
sit down," Dr. Pinker
said. His thin hair
was greasy and pushed
to one side. "How is your
leg?" I didn't know what
he meant. So
I said, "My thigh
is about one-quarter
the height
of my whole body."

Dr. Pinker
laughed the way kids
at school laughed, so
I said, "Stop."

Dr. Pinker
touched his jaw.
"Alex, I know
that we told you
you would be here
for a month. And
we would be doing
a lot of tests
to check
your progress—"

I nodded, knowing that this
moment was like
when you are at
the very top of
a very tall slide.

Enough Tests

Glen put his hand
on my shoulder and
squeezed. I wanted
to say, *Don't you
dare touch me.*

Dr. Pinker continued. "Well,
we have decided
not to have you come
back to Project Apogee
anymore."
I tried to make
my face do something.

Glen stood
over me. "Do you
get what's happening,
Alex? Your
parents are on
their way to
take you home."
I looked over
at Myra.

She looked
like someone
kicked her
in the gut.

Glen smiled a bad smile.
"What Dr. Pinker means
is that you finished
your work.
You don't
have to
come back here
and take a test
ever again.

You get
enough tests
at school. Am I right?"

These Things

"But what if I want
to come back
here?" I asked.

I thought
of Anto and
the stars
and my whole
blue life.

"We think it would be
best for you,"
Dr. Pinker said, "if
you tried not
to think
about Project Apogee.

Think of this
as another way
of learning
to control
your memory."

I thought of the
13 ceiling
lights on the way
from the blue room
to the common room.

I thought of the
27 to
29 drips
that fell after
every time
I turned off
the faucet in
the bathroom sink.

I focused
my eyes
on a tiny crack
in the window
of Dr. Pinker's lab
that grew
a little longer
every time
I saw it.

*I will never forget
these things.*

The Blue Sky

"But what did I do wrong?
I can try again," I said. I felt
hot tears and knew
my face was doing
something that
everyone could see.

Myra gave Dr. Pinker
a look and put down
her clipboard. She put
her arms around me. "Myra,
don't—" Glen said.

Dr. Pinker put his hand up.

No one said anything. I
let myself cry.
I filled up all
the silence
with my crying
sounds. I was not
embarrassed
because Myra
said, "That's OK,
that's
good, Alex."

They let me say goodbye.
But it was very
quick. In the common
room, I cried again.
And Anto gave me
a bracelet she
made out of the
purple strings
of a hammock
that hung
above her bed.

In the blue
room there was
a clear blue sky.

Outside there was
the same clear
blue sky. It was so
clear it made
me dizzy.

The Details

I didn't really
get it until
Anto explained it
to me
a month later
when she got home.

Words were
her gift.

I was in my treehouse
when my dad called
up to say Anto
was on the phone.

"You're so lucky,"
she said.

"How?" I asked.

"Don't you
get it? You're done
with this. I'll never
be done."

"So?" I asked. "They
didn't even let me
do the memory
tests over."

"That's not
why they kicked
you out, silly."
Anto understood
some heart things
much better than
I did. Even though
I was just as smart
as she was.

"It was your leg, and,
well, this is just a
rumor, but—
Ander said it's
because you're
too much
like a girl."

"Like a girl?"
I had never thought
of myself
that way before.

But
it felt good.

I did like all
the things girls liked.
And my only friends
outside the Nine were
girls. I liked the ways
I was sensitive. I liked
painting my nails.
I liked listening to glittery
pop music.

Being a Girl

I thought about being
a girl. And it was
like a little light
went on
inside my chest.

"I like the things I like,"
I said. "I like myself."

"I like you,
too," Anto said.
"Anyway, the whole
thing is genius.
You got out."

"Whatever," I said,
with the sourness
I had been holding
onto since I'd left.

"This is the first
time in your life
your body and mind
have just been yours,
Alex," Anto said.

My Body

When I left the Project,
I didn't have to do
memory stuff
anymore
on the
weekends.
But I also
didn't get
to see Myra.

I lost touch
with all
the Project kids
except Anto. She
sent me emails
from a fake
account called
freak0fnurture.

Anto always loved that
joke. The joke
of our lives.
How we come
from nowhere.

I always hated
that joke. Because
when you come
from nowhere, it's
too easy to send
you back.

My parents told me
that forgetting
Project Apogee
is part of the
agreement. I have to
move on, they said.

But it's me, so
I can never *really*
forget things.
Anyhow, now I know
I am lucky.

I get to like
myself
and my body
and my big
stormy brain.

I'm really into my
superpower.
And that it's just
mine. It's like I'm
more than one person.

Sometimes I feel
like I'm lots of people
at once. I'm a boy
and a girl and maybe
some other people, too.

Alex at 15

Turns out, I can do a lot.

Here's a list:
I can memorize
anything—
a picture or a book
in just
a few minutes.

I can remember
how to get
anywhere,
even places
on the map
I've never
seen in real life.

I can name every
little flower growing
in my city,
and I like to wear
flowy skirts with
peonies or crocuses
like the ones that
bloom first in spring.

I can listen
to a song
just once
and sing it
back
note for note.

I can cook
exactly
721
dishes without
looking
at a recipe.

I can make lots
of different looks
with makeup. Sometimes
I do glam rock and
sometimes I just
do regular.

I like
learning about
spices and herbs.
How to
combine
flavors to
make the most
delicious
mixes. It is a
skill and
an art.

Dizzy Spells

I have even
learned how
to use
plants I find
in the woods
to help with
the dizzy spells
that I go
through
every day.

When I feel
good, I can
focus my powers
and make
the spells even
stronger.

I can also make the
dizzy spells
go away if
I want. Which is
a good thing
when your
powers are the
difference between
being wanted
and not wanted
by the people
who made you.

When I wake up
from my dizzy spells
I think about
nothing. In my
head I make
a perfect blank.

This is my favorite
thing I can do. I
can change
my mind and
my body, too.

And that's
important magic.

I sent a whole
package of my
plant mixtures to
Anto.

She said they
did "amazing
things" for
her, too.

I can't wait
to hear more
about her
"amazing things."

A Perfect Subject

Sometimes when I'm
lying in bed before
I fall asleep now
I think about my life
in the blue room.

I think about Anto
and the others and Myra
and then
I think about one thing
Dr. Pinker told me
when he was buzzing
off my pretty long
hair before I left.

I was crying and he said
to me, "You
are a *boy*, a perfect
boy. You are a perfect
subject. You will
always belong to
Project Apogee."

I think about that
to. He said *to*. He did
not say *at*. I did not
belong at Project Apogee,
and I never would.

A Call from Myra

I got a call from Myra
yesterday. Mom
was worried
that I shouldn't
talk to her.
Because of how
the Project
treated me. But
Dad reminded her
Myra was always
on our side.

It has been almost
eight years
since we
spoke.
I never thought
I'd hear from
her again.

I haven't thought
about the Project
in a long time.

Myra said she missed me, so
I knew it was
okay to say,
"I miss you, too."

"Alex," Myra said.
"I have to tell you
something bad."

I was surprised, but
more than anything
I wanted to know
what Myra could have
to talk to me about.

"I wanted to warn you—
you are going to get
a call from Dr. Pinker,"
Myra said.

"Why does
Dr. Pinker want
to talk to me?"
I suddenly felt
scared and dizzy.

"Well, something
terrible has
happened," Myra said.
"Project Apogee
needs you."

They

"Absolutely not," Mom
said, cutting in. She was
listening on the phone in
the kitchen. Then Dad said,
"I don't understand." He was
on the phone in his office.

My parents were worried
for me. They did not
trust Dr. Pinker.

Years ago,
when I was kicked out
of the program,
they told me
they were glad. They didn't
think that Project Apogee
had my best interests
at heart anymore.

"You have lost
the right
to drag Alex
into the Project's
problems," Mom said.

"But he has to come back,"
Myra said.

"They," Dad said.

"What?" Myra said.
"Alex uses they/them pronouns
now. Which you would
know, if you had kept
in touch." Dad sounded angry.

"I'm sorry,"
Myra said.

Then quietly
Myra said, "*They*
have to come back."

My Job

"But why?"
I jumped in.

"I'm not allowed
to say," Myra said.

Dad laughed in kind
of a rude way.
Mom said,
"Well, you're
going to have
to tell us something
if you want
us to help you."

"I could lose
my job," Myra said.

"I thought it was
your job to be my
Monitor," I said.
I didn't mean to
sound mean. But
I've known
Myra since
I was born.

I used to think
her job was
to love me.
And then I thought
it was her job
to fix me. And
it was my job to
be perfect—
perfect for
Project Apogee.

Now I know
my parents love me,
which is not a job.

And I'm starting
to think it's my job
to fix Project Apogee.

The Nine at Fifteen

Here is what we know.

I am 15, almost 16,
years old. Which means
Project Apogee has been
running for exactly 15,
almost 16, years.

We are both teenagers, and
we are both a mess.

Because it is the end
of year fifteen, the Nine
(that is: Ander, Aggie,
Ashlun, Ace, Asa, Abel,
Ada, Alo, and Anto)
returned to Project Apogee
to be tested.

Dr. Pinker and Glen
and the other scientists
gave them
special tests
made for each
of their special
talents.

These tests
were harder
than the ones
when we were
seven. Even so,
Myra said, they
never expected
what happened next.

Total Loss

Every single Project kid
(that is: Ander, Aggie,
Ashlun, Ace,
Asa, Abel, Ada,
Alo, and Anto):
every one of them
failed their tests.

Aggie couldn't even
play the easiest musical pieces
they picked for her.

No matter
what the scientists
tried, Ashlun's
skin would
not clear up.

Ace couldn't
solve the number
puzzles she
made with
her Monitor
a year earlier.

Asa hurt himself
doing a simple
backflip. And
Abel caught the flu.

Ada took almost
the whole month
to beat
a new video game, with
help from her Monitor.

When Alo fainted in
the lab, and Anto
couldn't finish
a single poem,
Myra said
Dr. Pinker started
to panic.

And poor
Ander. They
couldn't get Ander
out of bed for testing.

All of their special
talents were gone.
Project Apogee had
created a bunch of
normal teenagers.

Myra called it a
Total Loss.

That's why Dr. Pinker
needed me to
come back.
I was the first kid
to disappoint
Project Apogee.

The first to fail.

The Missing Link

But my memory
was never a
problem. Myra
said that made
them surprised
and hopeful for
the future
of the Project.

Still, I was
the missing link:
the beginning
of the story of how it
all went wrong.

Not Going Back

I wanted to help Myra
but I was not going back
to Project Apogee.

That's what I told
Dr. Pinker and Glen
and the other
scientists. He offered
Mom and Dad
full tuition
to the college
of my choice.

He offered me a car,
anything I want.

"Come in and
I'll show you,"
he said. "We just
want to do
a few more tests."

But I knew better.

Nothing Special

It's like Anto said:
I just wanted to be
in control of my
own life, my own
body. I wanted what
every other teen had.

I wanted regular
boring rainy days
and clear blue skies
and nothing special.

Mom and Dad
said they were
proud of my choice.

They said I was growing
up. They liked
who I was
becoming and who
I was right then.

Whenever they
tell me they're proud
of me, that little light
in my chest feels
a little brighter.

One More Call

I was dreaming about
my blue room in the
Rainbow Ring at
Project Apogee. I was
dreaming about the
spaces between the
star patterns
on my ceiling.
And the
crack of light
under the door that
made the room even
bluer.

I was dreaming
blue dreams
when I got a
third call from
Project Apogee.

I knew it was
from the Project
because of the
blocked number.

I heard
a whisper voice.
And the whisper
voice was
crying. The
whisper voice
said, "Alex,
help us."

The Nine in Trouble

It was Anto. She had
broken into Glen's
office. I was so happy
to hear from her. And
so worried for
her and the others.

"I can't really
talk," she said.
"Just listen."

"They are keeping us
here. They don't want
anyone to know that
we all failed the tests.
Dr. Pinker won't let
us go or see our families
until we get better.

But Alex," she said,
"what if we never
get better?"

I thought for a minute. I never
got better—at least I
never got better in the
way Project Apogee
wanted me to.

I never wanted
Dr. Pinker to know
about what
I could do during
my genius headaches,
my dizzy spells.
Because I was
worried that
they would never
let me see Mom
and Dad again.

They didn't know
what I could see
or how I saw it.
Something like memory,
but bigger.

As big as the world.

But I had to go back
to Project Apogee.

I made a promise
to Anto. She told me
she had also been
in touch with her
grandmother. She
always knew what to do.

Dr. Pinker's First Mistake

When the Nine failed
to make progress,
the first thing
the scientists did was
blame the parents.

They called all
the parents and
told them they would
be asked lots of
questions. About their
homes and the way
they lived.

Parents were told
their kids
would be living
back at Project
Apogee for now. And
if they didn't
go along with this, they
might lose
their kids forever.

It was sort of like
when they threatened
me and my parents.
But at least
we were allowed
to stay together. This
was much worse.

It was about control.
Project Apogee
needed to get back
in control. That's
what Mrs. Rodriguez,
Anto's grandma, said
when Mom and Dad
invited her over
for coffee.

She was organizing a
support group for the
families of Project
Apogee kids. And
she hoped my
parents would join.

Bullies

Even though
I hadn't left yet,
my parents were
already so sad.

I didn't understand
a lot of what they
talked about. But
I did hear Mrs. Rodriguez
say, "I have a plan to
bring them home" and
"how dare they bully us."

I knew about bullies.
Mom and Dad
always said they
try to scare people
because they're
scared.

So maybe
Dr. Pinker was
scared of us.

Back to the Lab

I packed very little to
go back to my blue
room at Project Apogee.
My favorite socks,
drawing pencils, some
herbs. And a book about the
science of dreaming
and the brain.

I was looking
forward to being
with my
blue room stars.
And I couldn't wait
to see the other
Project teens.

I didn't want to
leave my school.
And I didn't want
to leave Mom and Dad.
And I really didn't
want to go back
into the gross lab
and take tests all
day again.

I didn't want
to share
my superpower
with them.
I didn't
want them
to own me again.

But more important
than any of those
things was the
fact that Anto
and the rest
of the Nine
needed me now.

Last time I was at
Project Apogee, I
was just a little kid.
I didn't know
anything about
myself. I didn't know
anything about us.
The power of an "us."

This time would
be different. In a way,
Dr. Pinker and
the government
scientists and I
were not so different.

We were worried
about being
embarrassed. We
were worried that
the things we
cared about the
most would
be taken away
from us. We wanted
to be recognized.

I didn't
hate them.

I just wanted
to belong
to myself.
I wanted
to love
what I love.

Strong in My Body

I got to the gate
at the front of
Project Apogee. And
I got this big mixed-up
feeling in my body
of fear and *wow* and *run away*
and *heavy*, then *strong*.

I was ready.
Dr. Pinker met me
at the door. He shook
my hand, which was
weird. It was also weird
that he looked happy
and angry at the
same time.

Myra met me at
the door, too. She put
out her arms. I let
her hug me. And I heard
her say softly right
next to my ear,
"I'm so sorry."

I was scared of what
she was apologizing
for.

If it was
for something I
didn't know
was about to
happen to me
again.

The Gray Room

Myra walked me past
the hallway that led to
the Rainbow Ring.
Into an area
I had never seen
before. She
punched in
a code to open
the door to the room.
Then she said, "This
is your room."

"No," I said. "My
room is blue."
I looked up at
the ceiling. Which
was completely
blank, white, clean.
No clouds. No stars.

There was a gray
bed in the corner
with a gray
blanket. On the
bed was a boy's gray
T-shirt. A pair
of gray sweatpants.

"No," I said.
"No, no, no,
no, no, no, no, no."

"Alex, I know
this is not what
you want. But
we have our
reasons," Myra said.

I snapped
out of it. "Fine," I
said. "But I brought
my own clothes."

"Come on, kiddo," she said.
"It won't be so bad."

Myra hadn't called
me kiddo in so long.
She picked up the
pants. Handed
them to me. "These
are very cozy."

"Whatever," I said.

"Well," I said,
taking off my
shoes. "When
do I get to see
the others?"

"What?" Myra
said. "The
others?"

"Yeah, will I
see them
at dinner?" I
watched Myra's
face change.

"I'm sorry, Alex.
The others aren't
here," she said.
"They were
sent home."

When Myra left,
the door locked.
And I stayed in
the gray room for
the rest of the night.

Someone brought
a tray, but I
was not hungry.

I woke up sometime
before the morning
and wondered
if Anto had
tricked me. Maybe
they had gotten to her.
I refused to
believe it. Maybe
something had
happened.

Wake Up

In the morning, the gray
room, which had no
windows, began to flash
with bright light.

A voice came through
a speaker
in the corner
above the bed. "Alex,"
the speaker said. "Wake
up. When the door
opens, you will go
to the lab for your
first test." I
recognized
the voice. It was
stupid Glen.

And sure enough,
when the door opened,
he was standing there.
"Morning, sport," Glen
said. "Ready to
show us your stuff?"
I shrugged.

When we got to
the lab, I stopped.
"I'm not going in,"
I said.

"I'm sorry?"
Glen said.

"I'm
not going in until
you tell me
what happened
to the others."

Glen looked at
me like I was
joking. "Nothing
happened to the
others. They went
home. They
finished their tests."

"You're lying,"
I said. I felt
hot. I turned
back toward the gray
room and screamed,
"STOP LYING TO ME!"

Nothing Bad

Just then, the lab doors
opened and Myra
and Anto's Monitor
came out into
the hall. I saw
Dr. Pinker
sitting at his
desk behind them.

"It's okay, Alex.
Nothing bad is
going to happen,"
Myra said. "You
remember Anto's
Monitor, right?" I
looked at them and
felt dizzy.

Then
I opened my eyes
and I was on the floor.

Oh no.

*I'm having
a genius headache
right in front of
the enemy.*

I had been practicing hiding
them. But
I couldn't
control myself
this time. It was
happening and
there was nothing
I could do about it.

I stood up
out of my body. And
walked right out
of the building and
into the air. I flew
over the military
base where Project
Apogee stood
and tried to see
my parents' house.

Before I knew it, I was
back in my body.
Blinking and breathing
on the exam table
in Dr. Pinker's lab.

Myra's voice came through.
"Don't worry, Alex."
I felt a cold hand
on my forehead.

"Easy does it," said Dr. Pinker's
voice from somewhere.

Then his face got very
close to my face, and
he said, "So, where did
you go?"

The First Test

I sat up too fast. I
felt dizzy and put
my head back down.

"You—you know
that I go places?"
I asked. I couldn't
believe it.

"Yes, of course.
That was your
first test," said
Dr. Pinker.

"Yes,"
Myra said. "And
you did a fantastic
job."

I felt like I
was going to
throw up.

My superpower,
my one special
thing, was
already theirs.

"But how did you
know?" I asked.

"Oh, Alex," said
Dr. Pinker. "We
caused you to have
that reaction."

"W—What?"

I looked
to Myra for some
kind of help. "The
light," Myra said.
"The light in your
room this morning."

I didn't know what
was real anymore
and what was
in my head.

I mean,
I didn't know what
was mine and
what was theirs.
The story kept
changing.

A Gray Visitor in the Gray Room

I barely slept that night.

In the moments when
I did sleep,
I dreamed I was
falling
into a well
that never ended.

I turned over and
over. Trying to
get comfortable.

I hate crying. But
I kept
crying on this
gray pillow
in my horrible
gray room.

I wiped my eyes
and saw a light
under the door
just like the light
I used to watch
for in my old
blue room.

I heard someone
punch in the door code.
And wondered if I
was still dreaming.

The door opened
very slowly, but
there was no one
there—

Or, at first,
it looked like there
was no one there.

I sat up in bed. On
the floor rolling
toward me was
Ander's robot
from the red room.

I moved toward
the robot carefully,
trying to not
scare it away. Or
maybe I didn't
want to wake up
from whatever
dream I was
having.

Then I heard
the robot say,
"Knock knock."

An Old Joke

"Who's there?"
I asked.

"Us,"
the robot said.

Nothing happened.

"Us who?" I tried.

A little red light
in the middle of
the robot's face
blinked on.

"Don't worry, Alex,"
it said. "We're all
getting out of here
for good."

Good and Evil

That's how I knew
the Nine were still
somewhere at
Project Apogee. Anto
hadn't lied to me
at all. Myra had.

Knowing that
Myra had been
lying to me hurt
me just as much.
Maybe there is
no way of ever
knowing who is
your friend and who
is pretending.

I don't believe
in good
and evil. I
believe in
different kinds
of scared and
who chooses
to do what is hard
even though
it scares them.

The Nine were
there with me.
I felt hope
come up in me
like an idea.

Maybe
they were all being
kept in gray
rooms, too.

Who's There?

"Who's there?"
I asked.

"Ada," the
robot said.

I laughed
and asked, "Ada who?"
even though I
was pretty sure
I knew Ada who.

"Ada and Alo and Ander."

I was so glad
to hear these names.
"AND ANTO," the
robot added
after a second.

"Where are
you all?"
I asked.

"Knock knock," the
robot said. I realized
that I had to
complete the joke
to hear from
the Nine again.

The robot had only
ever spoken in
knock-knock jokes
when it lived
in the red room
with Ander.

"Okay. Who's
there?" I asked.

"The common
room," the robot
said. I wondered
why Dr. Pinker
would be keeping
the Nine there.

"The common
room who?"
I asked.

The Plan

"The common room
is set up with
all the beds
like a dorm,"
the robot said. I
thought about how
nice it was that
at least they're
all in there
together. Then the
robot said,
"Yeah, a really
shabby dorm."

I laughed and
it felt like
the best thing
I'd ever felt.

"Knock knock,"
the robot said again.
"Who's there?"
I asked. Then
the robot said,
"The plan."

"The plan
who?" I asked.

"The plan
is you,"
the robot
said.

The Robot's Promise

The robot told me
about how we
were going to
trick Dr. Pinker's
team. It told me
how we
would try to
leave in
two days.
Which the robot
told me
was how long it
would take
for our allies
on the outside
to prepare
a safe house.

Finally, it told me
what exactly
the Nine meant
by telling me
I was the plan.

I had to play
along with
Dr. Pinker's
plot. Whatever
it was. I had to
keep letting them
test me and
make me have
genius headaches.

The plan was
a good plan.

But I couldn't get one
thing out of
my head.

"So you did
try to get me to
come back so
you could
use me to
escape?" I
asked. "And
I just have to
stay here and
let them do
this?" I was
crying again.

I didn't know if
they would be
able to hear me
cry or not. But
I didn't care.

"I'm sorry,
Alex," the robot
said, after I asked,
"Who's there?"

"I'm sorry,
it's me." I knew it
was Anto. "We had
to do it this way.
You're the one they
want now. But
we'll make it
up to you. I
promise."

I had no idea
what time it was.
But talking
through knock-
knock jokes took
what felt like
a long, long time.

I didn't even have
time to fall back
asleep before
the lights in
my room
flashed on
again.

"Alex, wake up,"
said the voice
from the speaker.

"I'm awake,"
I said. And I
meant it.

That morning
I could feel
my genius
headache coming.
Which was still
a little scary. But
I could feel
something else,
too. There it was—
hope, an idea.

Dr. Pinker's Second Mistake

From Dr. Pinker's exam
table, I climbed up out
of my body. Like
I had always done
during my
spells. But this
time I knew
what I was
looking for.

Instead of walking
out of the building
and into the air,
I simply walked
down the hall.

I walked
into the common
room, where I
could see the Nine.
Anto with her dark curls
looked so cool and calm.
She had her arm around
Ander, whose tall,
muscular body slouched
into her. He
looked like he had
been crying. Ada
brushed her bangs
away from her face,
and even though
I knew she could
not see me, I thought
she winked.

Then I went
into the security
room. The two
security guards
watching the
cameras were
eating cheese
puffs and talking
about football.

I looked exactly
where Ada
told me to look
through the
robot. And there
was the folder with
the map of the
code patterns
for the doors
of Project Apogee.

Ada told me
the information
that I was looking
for was not the door
codes themselves.
But the pattern
that showed how
the codes changed
over time.

"Each door code
in Project
Apogee changes
every time any
door next to it
is unlocked. That's
how they keep
us in here," Ada said.
"They are always
one step ahead."

It took me the
entire time I
was out of my
body to memorize
the whole folder
of numbers.

Luckily I only
had to get back
to Dr. Pinker's
exam table by
the time I came
out of my spell.

And when I opened
my eyes, there he
was again, asking me,
"Where'd you go, Alex?"

"I went to the lake
by my house,"
I said, lying. "I like
to feed the fish."
Dr. Pinker pressed
his lips together.
He looked at me for
what felt like
too long.

His eyes
felt like lasers.

"Sounds nice," Myra
said, standing
behind him. Dr. Pinker
looked at her.
"Yes," he said.
"Funny how we
can go anywhere,
and we always
go home."

He wasn't wrong.
But he had just
let me wander
around Project
Apogee unsupervised.

And I realized
how many places
that I had seen
during my
genius headaches
also felt like
homes. Every
one of them,
my secret place.

The Robot Returns

That night the robot
came back to
the gray room, just
as it had before.
And it said:
"Knock knock."

I asked, "Who's
there?" Even though
I knew exactly
who was there.

Sometimes, even
when things are
very bad, all
of life just feels
like a really
good joke.

In order for me
to give Ada all
of the door code
information, she
had to first switch
who was telling
the knock-knock
jokes and who
was listening.

When Ada said
"Who's there,"
I would say the
area of Project
Apogee that
they would need
the code pattern
for. Like "The
Rainbow Ring."

Then Ada would
say, "The Rainbow
Ring who?" or whatever.
And I would say
107
numbers as
quickly as I could.

I didn't sleep much
that night
between all
the back and
forth with the
robot and me
worrying about
what was
about to happen.

The Last Morning

After my genius
headache on
Dr. Pinker's exam
table, I told him that
something had
happened during
the night.

"I woke up from
a dream in
the middle of
the night. And got
the same feeling
that I get
in the morning
when they flash
the lights."

"Interesting," said
Dr. Pinker. He turned
and looked at Glen and
then Myra. And they
all looked excited. I
hated making them
happy, even if it
was for a good cause.

"Then what happened?"
Glen asked, sitting
on the edge of
the exam table.
I wanted him
to get away
from me. "Please
move," I said.

"Oh," Glen said.
Myra moved
between Glen
and me.

And then
she asked, "Alex,
what happened
after you got the
feeling?" I didn't
want to like her,
but I couldn't
help it. Even
after everything,
I didn't want
to lie to her.

I gulped. "I had
a dizzy spell,
like the same
kind I have
in here."

Dr. Pinker made
a sign with his
hand for Glen
to go with him
over to the other
side of the room.

They talked for
a minute. And
Myra took my
hand and said,
"Alex, I just
want you to
know how proud
of you I am.
And how proud
of you your
parents are."

"Don't talk
about my
parents," I said.
It came out
louder than
I meant it to.
Myra pulled her
hand away.

Dr. Pinker came
over to me and
said, "Good news.
We're going to
go outside
today."

"Wow," I said.
"That's great."
It wasn't
bad news. It just
wasn't what I
was expecting.

"Yes it is," Glen
said. "This is
an exciting day
for all of us."

"And then tonight,"
Dr. Pinker said,
"we're going to
give you some
tests while you
sleep." There it
was. That's what
the Nine and I
had planned for.
I felt relief and
fear all at once.

Glen turned
to Myra, and said,
"And Myra will
stay over and sleep
right outside
the gray room!
Maybe you can
even watch a movie
together."

Dr. Pinker gave
Glen a look. And
then he asked, "Yes,
doesn't that sound
like fun?"

Before I
could say
anything, Myra
jumped in. "No,"
she said. "I don't
think that's
a very good idea."

Out

Glen looked
surprised.
And Dr. Pinker
barely looked at
her. He kept
smiling at me,
and said, "We
will talk about
this later."

"No we won't,"
Myra said. She
took off her gloves.
Glen said, "Myra,
you don't want
to do this."

She said, "I have
wanted to
do this for
months." Glen
looked like he
was going to
laugh or cry.

Just like that,
Myra was out.

And Out

That afternoon,
we went outside,
just as Dr. Pinker
said we would.

We took a car
to somewhere
off the interstate
highway. I sat
blindfolded in
the back seat the
whole way there.
The sun
was coming
through the
trees in slices.
That meant it
was mid to
late afternoon.

I know this
because of the
way the light
and shadow
flickered through
the cloth over
my eyes.

When the car
came to a stop,
Glen removed
my blindfold
and I got out
of the car. We
were deep in
the woods.

Dr. Pinker
was wearing a
goofy-looking
bucket hat.
He said,
"Let's
go for a little
hike."

Another black
car pulled up
right behind us.
Some of the
other kids'
Monitors and
a few other
scientists got
out of the car.

"Everyone needs
a day out in
nature every
once in a while,"
Dr. Pinker said.
He actually seemed
like he was having
a good time. He
never seemed nice
or cheerful in
the lab. I noticed
for the first
time that he looked
like someone's
grandfather.

We walked around
in the woods
all day. We stopped
for lunch. We
found old wasps'
nests and animal
tracks and ran
into some
wild turkeys.

It was so
strange to be
spending time
with Dr. Pinker
and the scientists.
Glen walked far
ahead of us.

On his own.

It gave me
the creeps.

For Smell

When we got back,
it was pretty dark.
Some of the
scientists helped
me get ready
for my next test.

They rolled a few
machines into my room.
I put on my gray
sweatpants and
got into bed. Before
he left for the
night, Dr. Pinker
took some of
the leaves and
pinecones from
the woods and
spread them out
on my nightstand.

"For smell," he
said, still smiling.

"What do you
mean?" I asked. "Do
you want me to
memorize the woods?"

Dr. Pinker said, "I
think you can
go back and find
the exact same spot
in the woods where
we went today.
I want you to try."

But I couldn't do it.

No way.

I had never tried
to land somewhere
so particular that I
had never seen on
a map. What if
I failed again?

Wow, I thought,
why do I still care
what they think
of me? Why am I
still trying to
impress Dr. Pinker?

I got angry
with myself
for being
such a big baby.

Getting Dizzy

Back at Project
Apogee, it was
easier to remember
why the whole Project
made me feel
so tired and sad.

Glen attached some
colorful wires
to my head.
He took his
post outside the
gray room.

They actually let me
watch a movie.

Glen told me that
the movie would
help me feel dizzy.
The way the flashing
lights made me feel
in the mornings.

Before I put
my head down,
I felt a tiny piece
of paper under
my pillow. It said:
*I'm sorry. I will
always be here
for you.
Love, Myra*

Focus

The movie was
like a comic book.
Lots of black
and white cartoon
animals chasing
each other and
flickering scenes.

It did make
me feel dizzy,
just like Glen said.
But I needed to
focus in order to
make myself
have a powerful
dizzy spell. The
kind that the Nine
needed me to
have for their
plan to work.

I had given the Nine
all the information
Ada needed to
get them out. But
now I needed to
do something
even harder. I
needed to make
Project Apogee
go completely dark.

I closed my eyes
and focused. I could
smell the wet leaves.
I felt dizzier and
dizzier, but I didn't
stop. I went deeper
into the back of
the blue room
inside my head.
It seemed to go
on forever. Darker
and darker, like
a blue cave.

I saw another Alex
in there. And then
another Alex. Then
more Alexes. I
followed them
through the blue.
Or maybe they
followed me.

I felt my body
shaking and my
eyes rolling.
I kept going farther
inside, farther than
I had ever gone.
I didn't stop, even
when I felt afraid.

And that's when
it happened. A huge
light exploded on the
outside. But I was
so deep inside, I
could barely see
the sparks. Wherever
the Nine were now,
the night was theirs.

The Woods

In my spell,
I found the woods
that Dr. Pinker wanted
me to find. It was easy enough.
The smell led me to
remember this one
creek near Project
Apogee, which led to
a bigger stream. And
then I was not so far
from where we
started hiking
between the river
and the highway.

I floated around there
for a little while, and
then I realized something:

I didn't have to prove anything.

The point of this was
to get the Nine out.
Who cares if I did
what Dr. Pinker
wanted? This was
my show now.

When I came back
to my body, I saw
what I had done.
And I was prouder
of myself than
I've ever been.

All of Project
Apogee was dark.
There were voices
screaming in the
hallways. The doors
were all open.

In the common room,
the Nine were gone.

When the lights
came back on,
I saw Glen run
through the doors
to Dr. Pinker's lab,
with his cell phone
to his ear. He was
especially upset. I
think probably
because he would
be blamed for this.

Alone

I wasn't out
of my body
long enough to
get to see where
the Nine went
once they left
Project Apogee.

But they had
a plan for what
would happen next.

After the rush of
the escape, and
all the noise
around the gray
room, I didn't
realize I would
feel depressed
again so fast.

I realized I
didn't know
what was going
to happen to me.
Just like always.

There it was,
the same old
fear. The same
old alone.

Project Apogee
was the starting
point for all of my
aloneness.

Whether I was
there or not—
I would always
be alone.

I tried to feel
happy for the Nine.
But more so, I felt
hurt that they
left me here
alone. Just like
Myra and my
parents and everyone
I thought had ever
loved me.

I pulled the busted
wires out of my
hair and threw
them on the floor.

Then I curled up to
wait for whatever
terrible thing
was coming for
me next.

The Last Last Morning

When I woke up, there
were no flashing lights.
But the door was
closed and locked.

I looked up at the
speaker. "Hello?"
I asked. Nothing
happened.

I got dressed and
stood at the door.
I sat on the bed
and waited. I was
wondering if
with the Nine
escaping in the
middle of the night,
they had forgotten
about me. And then
I heard someone
putting in the
door code.

One of the scientists
pushed open the
door. And then
from behind her
white lab coat,
I saw them.

They came
rushing in with their arms out.
And I ran to them.
And it was like
one of those
moments you
always see in
the movies. It
felt like the
best dream I
could ever
have in that
dull gray
room.

It was
my parents.

Reunion

When we walked out
together, I noticed
that Project Apogee
was completely empty.
I didn't see Glen or
most of the other
scientists there.

One or two guys in
brown clothes were
checking switches
and cameras and things
like that. But Dr.
Pinker was not around.

My parents told me
when we got to the
car that they were
so sorry they let
me go back into
that place.

"It's okay,"
I said, even though
I remembered how
alone I'd felt the
night before.

We drove for a long
time. So long
I fell asleep in
the car.

The sun had
already tipped
over to the
other side of
the sky, which
meant it was afternoon.

I looked
at the clock, and it
said 2:20. I asked,
"Do you know
what happened
to them?" The
car stopped. Dad
turned around
and said, "See
for yourself."

We pulled up to a big
house in the
middle of a field
with woods all
around us. The big
blue front door
of the house opened.

And there were
Ada, Ander, Alo,
and Anto, running
toward me.

We hugged and hugged.
We laughed and
kicked the dirt. We
looked around
at the big blue
sky and the trees.
We took big
breaths of fresh air
and talked about
the night before.
And we talked about
that morning.

The morning
everything changed.

Ada told the story
of how she used
the robot to set
the door codes,
each door triggering
the next door
and the next door
after that, like
dominos.

Ander and
Alo made sure
cameras were out
and the halls were
clear. Anto led the
rest of the Nine
out of the common
room, out the doors
of Project Apogee
and through the
base. To the vans
waiting to take
them here.

"The vans?" I asked.
"Yeah," Anto said,
her dark eyes
on the trees behind me.
"My grandmother
and some of
the parents in
the support group—
they got the vans
together and found
this old farmhouse."

The Others

Anto pointed to her
grandmother, who
was moving slowly
toward us with
her walker.
I had only met
her once. But
I was so happy to
see her, I gave her
a big hug. "Hi again,
Alex," she said. "You
didn't think we'd
leave you there all
by yourself with
the bullies, did you?"
She smiled.

"No," I said. I blushed and
laughed at the
same time. Because
I did think that, but
I was so glad to be
proved wrong.

"What about the
others?" I asked. Mom
put her arm around
me. "Their parents
were worried about
coming up here. And
they wanted to stay
in their houses. We
tried to convince them,
but you can't make
people do something
just because you
think it's right."

I looked down at
the dirt, and my
chest got really tight.

"So we won't
see them
ever again?"
I asked.

"Well, who knows?"
Anto's grandmother said.

Dad said, "Yeah, maybe
they'll change
their minds and
come up later."

"The point is,"
Alo said, "we're
together, and we're
safe." He looked
back to the house,
where two people
and a little kid
looked back at him
and waved.

"Are those your parents?" I asked.

"Yeah," Alo said, "and
my little brother.
I can't believe they're
here. I can't believe
any of us are here."

"Sure you can," Ada
said, laughing. "You're
the one who
never stopped fighting
Dr. Pinker." She turned
to me. "They locked him
up alone in a room,
like you. He went
on hunger strike."

Alo shrugged. "It
wasn't a big deal,"
he said. "You know
I don't need to
eat." My eyes got
really big and I looked
at the two of them. "So
that means—" I said.

Still Got It

"Yeah," Alo said. "Didn't
Anto tell you? We've
all still got it. I mean,
Ada would have never
been able to get us
out of there if she
couldn't code."
Ander handed me the
red robot. "We would
have never been
able to use this little
guy to talk to you."

"Yeah," Ada said,
popping Ander in
the shoulder. "You
would have never
figured that out.
Without me, you'd
still be in the common
room answering knock-
knock jokes in French."

"Right? It's so funny
Dr. Pinker thinks we
all just somehow
lost our abilities,"
Ander said. "A stroke
of genius from Anto
for sure."

"What?" I asked.

"Oh, come on.
Tell them already!"
Ander said to Anto.

Anto grinned. Turned
to me. And said,
"This is all because of you."

Young Witch

"But I didn't even
know what was
happening," I said.

"It was the herbs!" said
Ander, before Anto
could open her mouth.
"Anto said you sent
her that plant mixture."
I must have looked
confused. Because
Alo said, "You
made it, right?"

"We all took some,"
Anto said. "And
it helped us hide our powers."

"It was Renée and
Anto's idea," Mom said,
looking at Anto's
grandmother.

"When Anto told me
what you were
doing with these
plants, I thought,
wow, a young witch
friend for me," said
Anto's grandmother,
whose name was
Renée, which sounded
like bells and
violins and dessert. *Renée.*

Changing Our Minds

Renée said
I was a witch,
like her. I
loved that. So much
new information.
My head
was buzzing.

"We had to practice
at first," Ander said.
"But after a while
we could all control
our abilities like magic.
For example,
when I eat some,
things feel really
dark and gloomy,
and I can't move."

Ada looked from
Ander to me, "He
just gets depressed,"
she said.

"Just?" Ander
said. "It feels
like the world is over."

Ada said, "Well, when
I eat some, my brain
scrambles. I can't even
use a graphing calculator!"

"There is so much
happening," Dad said.
"Why don't we go
inside and take
a break."

"But wait,"
I said. Mom and Dad
looked at each other
and laughed.

I always have
more questions.

The Biggest Surprise of All

Inside the farmhouse,
it was bright and warm.

People were sitting
around a fireplace
talking. There was
a big television
playing a news channel.
Mom and Dad
motioned for me to
go over. I was tired.

I had already
had the biggest
day of my life.

Dad said,
"Alex, look
who's here."

Myra didn't say
anything at first.
But she did stand up,
so I could see that
everyone was okay
with her being there.

Something felt
different. She didn't
seem like the Myra
I had been talking
to at Project
Apogee.

This Myra seemed
calmer, nicer,
like the Myra
I knew from
the blue room.

The Myra that
used to come
over on weekends.

Myra

I didn't go over
to Myra. And Mom
must have noticed
I was nervous
because she said,
"We would have
never gotten you
out of Project Apogee
today without Myra."

I looked at Myra.
"I wanted," she said,
so quietly I could
barely hear her, "to
help you. I wanted
to change things."

"She called us
yesterday," Dad said.
"She had no idea
what you kids
were up to."

"I just wanted
Dr. Pinker to
pay for what
he was doing
to you," Myra said.

Okay Soon

"He's just a bully,"
I said.

"Yes,"
she said. "I'm
sorry."

"It's okay,"
I said, because
that's what you say.

Plus I was starting to
feel like it might
actually be okay soon.

The Best Thing

"It's on!" Alo said.
"Turn it up," Anto said.

"What's going on?"
I said, looking around.

"The best thing,"
Renée said. "The best."

Breaking

Breaking News:
Today a secret
government
organization has been
uncovered by an
inside source as
a cruel and violent
prison for the
gifted children it
claimed to be
educating.

The organization is
called Project
Apogee. It is
now closed for
investigation.

Just then everyone
looked at Myra
and smiled.

The families
cheered
and clapped
and hugged
each other.

And it was then
that I understood
what Myra
had done
for us.

Free

That night
in our room,
in my own flower-patterned
pajamas, Dad
said, "Alex, we have
something to
tell you."

"No," I said. "Please
no more things.
I'm tired of new
things."

Mom laughed, but
it wasn't funny.
"I'm sorry, but we
have to talk to
you about leaving
tomorrow."

"LEAVING?" I
shouted. "We
can't go. We just
got here!"

"It's not safe," Dad said.

"Alo said we were
all safe here," I said.

"*You're* not safe. Because
Dr. Pinker and the other
scientists still think
you're the only one
who made it. They
will keep trying
to find you. Because
you are proof that
Project Apogee
worked."

Alone Again

Mom smoothed my
hair. "They won't
stop looking for
us. That's why
we have to leave."

Just like before,
I'd be the first
one out.

And I'd
be alone
again.

Goodbyes

Anto knocked on
the door and opened
it a little bit. "I'm
sad you have to leave
too, Alex," she said.
"But this is the only
way you can be
safe right now. Safe to
be yourself. All of
your selves. You're
special, Alex. But it's
important to know
you're not the only
one out there who
isn't exactly one thing
or another. There
are other people out
there for you and
there are other
people who need
your help. Go find
them. Remember we said
we'd make it up
to you?"

She was right.

I cried and she cried.

And my parents cried.

And the next day
everyone else cried,
too.

Because we all
deserved to feel
that feel-good thing
when you're done
crying for a while.

We packed up the car
and we drove over
the border. The other
side was beautiful.

We did not say
any goodbyes.

WANT TO KEEP READING?

If you liked this book, check out another book
from West 44 Books:

YOU AND ME AND MISERY
BY RAYEL LOUIS-CHARLES

ISBN: 9781538382776

I Think...

I'm falling in love. But, how can I be sure about her if I'm not even sure about myself?

Check out more books at:
www.west44books.com

An imprint of Enslow Publishing

WEST **44** BOOKS™

About the Author

Rye Duran is a trans writer and multidisciplinary artist from Atlanta, Georgia. Duran studied creative writing at University of Massachusetts Amherst and has been nominated for the Pushcart Prize. Duran's fabulist hybrid-genre work has appeared in *Ninth Letter*, *Salt Hill*, and *Bat City Review*. Favorite authors include Octavia Butler and Matthew Salesses.